QUENTIN QUIRK'S MAGIC WORKS

ATTACK OF THE BUM-BITING SHARKS

MATT KAIN

ILLUSTRATED BY

MACMILLAN CHILDREN'S BOOKS

For Kevin, and little brothers everywhere - MK
In loving memory of Nan and Da - JF

First published 2009 by Macmillan Children's Books
a division of Macmillan Publishers Limited
20 New Wharf Road, London N1 9RR
Basingstoke and Oxford
Associated companies throughout the world
www.panmacmillan.com

ISBN 978-0-330-51021-9

1 3 5 7 9 8 6 4 2

A CIP catalogue record for this book is available from the British Library.

Printed and bound in the UK by CPI Mackays, Chatham ME5 8TD

CONTENTS

CHAPTER ONE
JEZ LLOYD

From the bathroom window, Jez heard crunching on the driveway outside. He hurled himself down the stairs and threw the front door open. He was sprayed with gravel as Charlie skidded his Beemo to a halt.

'Ebo, Sharli,' said Jez. He sounded funny because he had a toothbrush sticking out of his mouth.

Charlie smiled. 'Hiya.'

'Coo skig,' added Jez admiringly. With his new birthday Beemo he'd be able to wreck the driveway too. He could hardly wait.

They were going to ride into town so that Jez could spend his £20.23 birthday money (the 23p was from his grandma, who'd never liked him). That was easily enough to buy things for the Beemo. Cool things like stickers and lights and mirrors and peggies and spoki-dokies.

Jez rinsed his toothbrush under the kitchen tap, hid it behind some broccoli to save going back upstairs and shouted, 'See ya, Mum!' Then he bolted out the door and leaped on to his brand-new bright blue Beemo Super X.

'Yee-hah!' he yelled, and they were off.

At the centre of Oakwood town there was a row of shops. If you weren't really paying attention, you might think it was just one long street. But actually it was two short ones.

Sheek Street ran in from the east, and Bleak Street ran in from the west. They met slap, bang, shamboozle in the middle of town. Jez and Charlie hung out in Sheek Street all the time, but they'd never dared go down Bleak Street. Not even once.

In Sheek Street the boys looked in Faberelli's Deli, Jameson's Fine Sausages, Trim's Barber's Shop, Portia's Poodle Parlour, Hattie's Hats and the Clock House. So far, the trip had been a complete disaster. Now they sat in Mrs Cappuccino's Cafe, sipping blueberry-and-banana

smoothies
through
green and
gold stripy
straws.

'Well,
we've looked
everywhere,' sighed Jez, 'and found
nothing. I don't want socks or sausages or a
lump of Brie or a haircut. And there isn't a
bike shop.'

'These smoothies are good though,' said
Charlie, taking a long slurp.

'Yeah, but I've still got fifteen pounds
forty-seven left,' moaned Jez. 'What are we
going to do with it?'

Charlie's eyes slid to the rich brown gooey
dessert behind the glass counter. 'Five helpings
of sticky toffee pudding?' he suggested.

'Char, you know how that stuff sticks your teeth together. We'd be trying to prise our jaws apart all afternoon! But listen – I've got a better idea.'

Charlie leaned in close over the table and tried to look interested. This was difficult, because his eyeballs seemed to be magnetically attracted to the sticky toffee pudding behind the counter.

'We'll go and buy something in Bleak Street,' Jez whispered.

Charlie was horrified. 'No way, Jez. It's *dangerous* down there.'

'True. But that just makes it more exciting.'

Charlie gulped. Bleak Street was dead scary. It was somewhere you just didn't go – not if you were sensible, anyway. And if Charlie was anything, he was sensible.

'No way, Jez,' he said firmly. 'I am

absolutely putting my foot down. I am *not* going down Bleak Street. Not now. Not ever. Not in a million years.'

Jez and Charlie coasted down Bleak Street. Charlie suddenly skidded to a halt and stared into the Greasy Spoon Cafe, pretending to be interested in the torn, stained notice in the window. Really he was trying not to go any further from the safety of Sheek Street. 'Breakfast menu,' he read. 'Soggy bacon, hard fried eggs, burnt sausages, rubbery toast, tea that tastes faintly of washing-up liquid. Three pounds fifty.'

'Yuck! No wonder the place is empty,' cried Jez. 'Maybe all the customers died of food poisoning and their bodies are—'

'Shut up!' hissed Charlie. 'You're giving

me the creeps. I don't know how you talked me into this!'

'Oh, chill out,' called Jez, setting off down the hill again.

Charlie sighed and followed. He couldn't let Jez go alone. Together they freewheeled past a couple of betting shops, a second-hand record store, Tony's TV Repairs and loads of empty units plastered with old posters. Suddenly Jez spotted something and braked hard.

Charlie smacked right into the back of him. 'Ow!' he yelled.

'Quirk's,' Jez whispered.

CHAPTER TWO
QUIRK'S

Charlie stared up at the faded sign on the rundown little building in front of them. He didn't like the look of the place. Not one little bit. A gang of greasy bikers hung out by the graffiti-covered wall opposite. They made him nervous. 'Nice wheels,' said the greasiest one, and the others sniggered at the Beemos. 'Come on, Jez. Let's go back,' Charlie hissed. 'This street's really dodgy. Besides, we don't even know what's in there.'

'It's just a shop,' said Jez, pressing his nose up against the window. A faded velvet curtain hung behind the glass, but there was nothing on display. 'Come over here – just for a look. We don't have to go in or anything.'

'Well, all right,' muttered Charlie, laying down his Beemo, 'but just for a look, OK?' He squished his nose up against the grimy glass. Through a tear in the curtain he could see inside. Dusty shelves stretched from floor to ceiling. They held rows and rows of bottles, jars, packets, cans, boxes and tins. 'It's weird in there, isn't it, Jez?' he whispered.

No reply.

Charlie spun round. Jez was no longer beside him. Instead, he was in front of the crumbling oak door. Knocking.

'Hey, you said just . . .' Charlie protested, but he fell silent as the door creaked open. They both looked up, startled. Towering over them was a very tall, very thin man. His frizzy black hair stood out as if he'd just been struck by lightning. When he spoke, his voice was crackly, like an old record player. 'Closed. Goodbye.'

'But the sign says: "Open",' Jez argued.

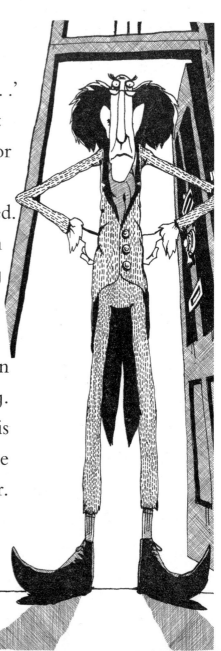

The man extended a long, bony hand. With the edge of a thick yellow fingernail he tapped the sign. 'Not any more,' he snarled. The word 'Open' shimmered silver, then became the word 'Closed'. Jez and Charlie gasped.

SLAM!

Wow, thought Jez. With the sign and everything, could this actually be a shop that sold *real* magic? 'Let us in!' he yelled, hammering on the door.

The door swung open again, and the shopkeeper glared down at the boys, eyes flashing with fury. 'WHAT DO YOU WANT?' he bellowed.

'We want to buy some magic,' said Jez. The shopkeeper laughed, tossing his head back. His thin neck creaked alarmingly. 'Ha ha ha! That's the funniest thing I've heard in a frightfully long time. *You* wish to purchase some magic?!'

'What's so funny about that?' asked Jez crossly.

'The very idea that I would sell magic to children, of course! That I, Quentin Quirk, voted Most Likeable Shopkeeper of 1894 by the Society of Evil Overlords, would do such a thing! It would mean breaking one of the most important rules in the Magic Works Owners' Handbook, section five, paragraph three! Not to mention the fact that I cannot stand sticky little brats anyway! Children *all* smell of salt-and-vinegar crisps. Children *all* have dried glue on their fingers. Children *all* wipe their noses on their sleeves!'

'We do not!' cried Charlie, amazed that a grown-up could be so rude.

But Mr Quirk didn't even hear him. 'Ha ha ha!' he laughed. 'Sell magic to *you*. The very thought!' He paused, pulled a black silk handkerchief from his jacket pocket and wiped the tears from his eyes. 'I'm sorry,' he said, in a not-sorry-at-all voice, 'but I don't serve children. Now, run along. GoodBYE.'

He began to swing the door shut. But Jez wouldn't give up. He just *had* to get into that shop. 'We've got money,' he shouted.

The door hovered ajar. Mr Quirk leaned into the street and sniffed the air. The tip of his long, pointed nose quivered.

'What are you doing?' asked Jez, puzzled.

'I'm checking whether you really do have money,' Mr Quirk explained. 'Money smells like a delicious ripe French cheese.' He sniffed the air again.

Jez and Charlie looked at each other, mystified.

'Ah, yes, you stink to high heaven,' concluded Mr Quirk.

'Charming,' said Charlie huffily.

Mr Quirk smiled like the wolf dressed as granny. 'Enter,' he said, ushering Jez and a reluctant Charlie into the dark, cavernous shop. 'Now then, what about a tin of today's special?' He gestured at a rickety table with a few dusty tins stacked up on it. *Today's Special.* The tins looked like they'd been there for 150 years. At least. The label on the top tin read: 'All-Seeing Shoe Polish'. Jez picked it up.

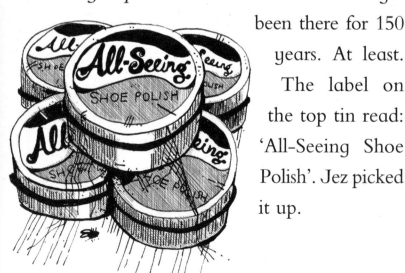

'Do NOT touch the merchandise!' shrieked Mr Quirk.

Jez placed the tin down gingerly, as if it was an unexploded bomb. 'What's it do, anyway?' he asked.

'Shine your shoes with All-Seeing Shoe Polish and you'll never step into a puddle or a pile of canine filth again,' said Mr Quirk proudly.

Jez looked puzzled. 'What's canine filth?' he whispered to Charlie.

'Dog poo,' Charlie murmured back.

'Oh! Erm, no thanks. What else have you got?'

Mr Quirk raised his eyebrows. He did *not* look impressed. 'At Quirk's, we stock a wide range of magical goods for the discerning professional,' he said haughtily. 'Dreams, hauntings, funny feelings, tricks.'

'Tricks?' Jez repeated. 'Oh good. We're looking for a trick to play on Francesca, my teenage sister. She's so moody and spiteful. Mum reckons it's just a phase but, personally, I think she's one of the demonic undead . . .'

'Don't speak ill of the undead,' snapped Mr Quirk. 'Some of my best customers are undead.'

'*Undead?*' spluttered Charlie.

'Sorry,' said Jez breezily. 'Anyway, what have you got to fix a wicked sister?'

'My tricks are far too good to be frittered away on *your sister*,' Mr Quirk hissed. 'Why don't you go to a children's joke shop? You could purchase some foaming sugar or fake blood or a whoopie cushion or some such item. This is a *serious* emporium full of *serious* magic.'

Jez could feel his temper rising. 'I'm

easily old enough to use serious magic, ta very much, and I . . .'

Mr Quirk held his hands up. 'Very well, very well. Don't have a tantrum!' His eyes flicked over the rows of potions on the back wall. 'As it happens, I have got something in stock that would fix a fearsome sister for a while.'

Charlie looked horrified. 'Jez,' he gasped, 'I know Francesca is a nightmare, but you can't use *magic* on her. That could be highly dangerous—'

But Jez had already made up his mind. 'We'll take it,' he said.

Chapter Three
Liquid Frighteners

Mr Quirk dragged a rickety stepladder over to the wall of shelves while Jez and Charlie inspected a few of the concoctions.

Jez noticed a packet of indigo powder and peered at the label: '"The Blues",' he read, '"One heaped teaspoon morning and night will cure you of excessive cheerfulness".'

'How much cheerfulness is excessive?' asked Charlie.

'*Any* cheerfulness,' said Mr Quirk darkly. He climbed up to the top shelf, knees creaking horribly, then reached across and

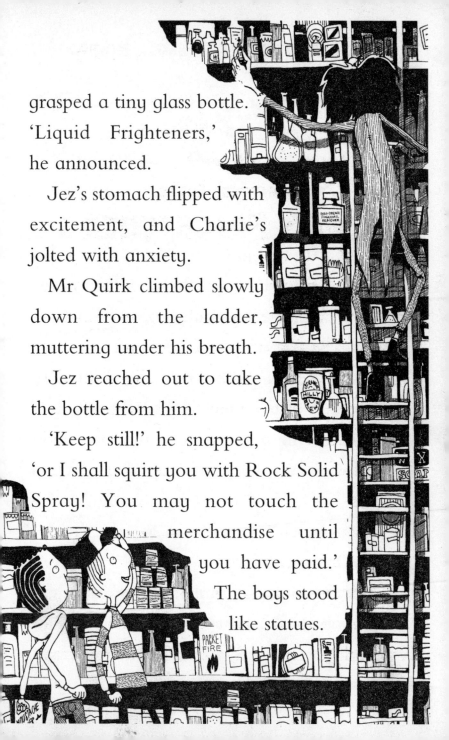

grasped a tiny glass bottle.
'Liquid   Frighteners,'
he announced.

Jez's stomach flipped with
excitement, and Charlie's
jolted with anxiety.

Mr Quirk climbed slowly
down   from   the   ladder,
muttering under his breath.

Jez reached out to take
the bottle from him.

'Keep still!' he snapped,
'or I shall squirt you with Rock Solid
Spray! You may not touch the
merchandise   until
you have paid.'
The boys stood
like statues.

'Well, how much does it cost then?' asked Jez, trying not to move his mouth.

Mr Quirk's left eye twitched. 'How much have you got?' he demanded.

'Fifteen forty-seven.'

'Well, that's most fortunate,' said Mr Quirk with a sly smile, 'because this potion costs exactly fifteen pounds and forty-seven pence. Pay now, please.' His hand sprung forward, palm up, like the drawer of a cash register shooting open. Charlie knew he'd just made the price up – nothing ever cost £15.47, because prices always ended in 99p – but he didn't dare say anything. Jez hesitated too.

'Well, the money! The money!' snarled Mr Quirk. 'Quick smart, boy! Do stop dawdling! Hand it over. However, please do not actually touch me with your greasy-crisp-eating, snotty-nose-picking little fingers.'

'There's n-n-no need to be so rude,' Charlie burst out suddenly.

Both Jez and Mr Quirk blinked at him in surprise.

'I mean, w-w-we don't even know what it does!' he continued, sort of wishing he hadn't started. 'It could be a con! Let's not buy it, Jez. Let's just get out of here! This p-p-place is giving me the jeebing heebies. I mean the heebing jeebies. I mean . . .'

Mr Quirk raised his eyebrows and rolled the tiny bottle around between his bony finger and thumb. The green liquid inside slid about tantalizingly.

'But, Char, what if the world's best trick is swilling around in that tiny bottle?' Jez whispered, without taking his eyes off the Liquid Frighteners. 'Besides, it's my money.'

Charlie shrugged. 'It's your funeral.'

'We'll take it!' said Jez firmly, handing over his notes and coins.

'Good,' said Mr Quirk, vanishing the money away like a conjuror. 'Please follow me to the sales desk.'

Mr Quirk steered Jez across the shop by the shoulder, then plonked him down on to one of the woodwormy chairs. Charlie went and sulked by the door.

'Now, I shall write down the instructions for you.' Mr Quirk opened the desk drawer and rummaged inside. He took out a yellowed scrap of paper, then opened a pot of purple ink, which he tipped and spilt all over it.

'Ooops,' said Jez.

A fleeting smile flickered across Mr Quirk's face. 'Observe,' he breathed.

Jez watched in amazement as the purple ink formed into words, leaving the rest of the paper clean and dry. 'Wow!' he gasped.

'Th-Ink,' Mr Quirk explained, looking very pleased with himself. 'You think words up; it writes them down. It is another of my *brilliant* inventions.'

The Th-Ink had written:

QUIRK'S
1 Bleak Street.

Liquid Frighteners x 1 (small)
Apply three drops twelve minutes
before the fright is required.

NEVER EVER PUT LIQUID FRIGHTENERS
INTO FOOD. DOING SO WILL
RESULT IN DIRE CONSEQUENCES
OF THE HIGHLY DANGEROUS KIND.

Mr Quirk rolled the paper up and secured it with an elastic band pulled from a huge knotted ball. 'Be sure to read these instructions carefully before use,' he warned Jez sternly. 'Please also note that Quirk's accepts no responsibility for any results or otherwise experienced while using our products. Nor do we offer refunds.'

He leaned over the desk, looked straight into Jez's eyes and dropped the bottle into his lap.

'Thank you,' said Jez.

'Thank *you*,' said Mr Quirk. 'Do come again. Or rather, don't!'

Then he snatched up a magazine and began to rifle through it, ignoring Jez completely.

Jez slipped the bottle into his pocket and hurried over to Charlie. When they got

outside, the greasy
bikers were gone.
Even so, they pedalled
like mad up the hill to
Sheek Street, not daring to look back. As
Charlie puffed and panted, trying to keep
up, he shouted to Jez, 'You know you can't
actually *use* it. You shouldn't do magic on
anyone. Not even Francesca!'

Chapter Four
Guess Who?

'Francesca! Francesca! Why are these towels on the bathroom floor?'

'Because they won't stick on the ceiling!'

This rude reply came from behind Francesca's locked bedroom door.

'Less of your cheek, young lady,' Mr Lloyd warned, 'or I'll come in there.'

'You wouldn't dare,' screeched Francesca.

Mr Lloyd decided that he didn't dare and stomped off downstairs.

By the way, Francesca is always in a right strop. That is perfectly normal. Francesca will be in a real stinker of a

stropaganza later in this story, but don't worry, you'll get some advance warning so you can cover your ears.

Francesca's bedroom was dominated by an enormous dressing table. It had a huge mirror with lights all around the edge. The top of it was covered in a clutter of half-used bottles of beauty lotions, grimy bits of cotton wool, spilt talcum powder and nail polish in twenty shades of pink. The floor wasn't much tidier. You could hardly move for high-heeled shoes scattered across every inch of the pink carpet.

There was a framed photograph by the side of Francesca's bed.

Now, most people have pictures of

their loved ones, so Francesca, as you can guess, had one of herself. All over the walls were posters of mega-hunks taken from her glossy teen magazines. Despite being vile, she behaved as if she was some sort of rare and exotic bird.

Francesca had been enjoying some important afternoon beauty sleep, but now she was on the prowl again. She slicked on some pink lipstick, sprayed herself with half a can of Boy Trap Body Spray, strapped on her spikiest shoes and headed outside. She hadn't been really nasty to anyone for three whole hours and it was giving her a headache.

Just then Jez and Charlie came skidding on to the drive, throwing wide arcs of gravel into the air which, unfortunately, missed Francesca.

'Oh, look, it's the two little losers,' she sneered, through a faceful of make-up. 'Where have you been?'

'As if we'd tell you,' said Jez with a scowl. 'Get lost, Francesca.'

'Ye-ye-yeah, get lost, Francesca,' stammered Charlie.

Francesca laughed a horrid glass-breaking laugh. 'Wow! Weedy Charlie standing up for himself. What a miracle! Careful you don't wet your pants, ickle boy.'

Charlie went bright red, and his hands clenched into fists by his sides.

'Lay off him,' warned Jez, squaring up to his sister.

'I . . . I . . . I . . . I . . .' stuttered Charlie. He was scared of Francesca in the way that little fluffy ducklings are scared of crocodiles.

'Ignore her – she's pathetic,' said Jez.

'If you children will excuse me, I'm off to meet Claudia and Jacintha,' said Francesca haughtily.

(Jacintha Arbuthnot-Smythe and Claudia Banshee were Francesca's best friends. They were only slightly less awful than Francesca herself. Jez called them the Three Witches.)

'Hubble bubble,' chanted Jez.

Charlie joined in. 'Toil and Trouble. Fire burn and cauldron . . .'

But Francesca didn't get annoyed. Instead

she smiled a smug smile, revealing lipstick-stained teeth. 'And I'm taking your iPod,' she said, pulling it from her bag and waving it at Jez.

'You are not!' he cried. But before he could reach her she'd tottered to the end of the drive. 'OK, I won't then, if you don't want me to,' she said sweetly. Then she opened the wheelie bin and dropped the iPod into it.

'Hey!' yelled Jez. As he made a lunge for her, Charlie ran to the wheelie bin and hitched himself up into it, leaning further and further in, trying to reach the iPod.

Francesca clawed at Jez with her super-sharp nails until he let go of her wrists, then she gave Charlie a sharp shove. 'Oops!' she cried, with a giggle.

'Aaaargh!' Charlie flipped over and crashed headfirst into the wheelie bin. The lid banged shut.

Francesca just laughed and tottered away up the hill.

'We'll pay you back, you nasty cow!' shouted Jez, eye-poppingly angry. 'We'll get revenge on you!'

Francesca turned on one sharp heel. 'Revenge on me? Dream on, bro, dream on!' She glanced over his shoulder and smirked. 'Oh, and maybe you'd like to give your dorky friend a hand. Busy road that. Bye!'

Jez spun round and gasped in horror. The wheelie bin was trundling away down Elm Hill, gathering speed with every second. It was heading straight for the busy junction.

'Hey, come back!' he shouted, streaking after it. Sprinting flat out, he caught up with it and threw himself on top. He could hear Charlie inside, shrieking and wailing in terror. He held on tight. Panic gripped him. They were nearing the junction, faster and faster and FASTER.

Just as they reached the lethal road Jez leaned hard left, forcing the wheelie bin sideways.

CLUNK! DOOOF!

The wheelie bin hit a tree and tipped over, sending Jez flying on to the grass verge. Charlie came spilling out and sat hugging a bin bag, staring at the roaring traffic crossing the junction.

Jez crawled to his side. 'You OK?' he panted.

Charlie looked down at himself. Luckily the bin bags (like giant cushions) had stopped him getting hurt. Unluckily lots of thick, slimy liquid from the bottom of the bags was oozing out all over his clothes.

He looked at the junction again, shuddering. 'You saved my life!' he gasped. 'Thanks, Jez.'

Jez shrugged. 'No probs. Maybe you'll do the same for me one day.'

'Doubt it,' Charlie muttered, staring at the grass, 'I'm not brave like you.'

'Yes, you are, Char. Just . . . in a different way, that's all.'

Charlie smiled, but he knew that Jez was just being kind. 'Err, gross!' he moaned, trying to brush the green slime, grey gloop and fish bones from his clothes (and making the mess worse). 'I can't believe she did that to me!'

'I can,' said Jez, his voice trembling with rage. 'I mean, she's like some mega-evil intergalactic death lord disguised as a teenage girl. But don't worry about my witch sister. We'll fix her.' He rummaged in his pocket and pulled out the little bottle.

As he waggled it at Charlie, the liquid inside slid about enticingly.

At that moment Charlie was so slimy and fishy and miserable that everything he'd said about not using highly dangerous magic on Francesca went out of his (gunk-covered) head. He looked at the bottle, then at Jez. 'Let's do it,' he said.

CHAPTER FIVE

FRANCESCA GETS THE FRIGHTENERS

Jez could hear the hot water pipes groaning and creaking in the loft. It was just after nine, and the bath was running. He lay on his bed with his door open, pretending to read a comic. Francesca pranced past in a pink dressing gown with feathers at the collar and cuffs. She had a mud pack on her face and some kind of conditioning gunk in her hair.

Jez stared intently at the page. He didn't want to attract her attention, not now. When he was sure she'd flounced back into her bedroom he put the comic down and took the Liquid Frighteners bottle out of his pocket. He grabbed a biro and made a few changes to the label. Then he crept across the hall.

Jez pushed the bathroom door closed behind him, then placed the little bottle on the side of the bath. *That should fix her*, he thought, grinning.

'A-HEM!'

Jez swung round to see a mud-faced Francesca standing, hands on hips, in the doorway.

'What are you doing in here, you little squirt?' she screeched. 'Get out! I need my privacy! It takes a lot of effort to look this effortlessly beautiful, you know!'

Jez grinned. He couldn't help it. Francesca certainly needed her beauty treatments. At the moment she looked like a flustered flamingo that had fallen face first into a cowpat.

'What?' Francesca demanded. 'What are you smirking at?'

Jez made a serious face. 'Nothing. Just getting my . . .' He groped around for the nearest thing he could find on the side of the bath. 'My, ah yes, my –' he read the label casually – 'unwanted hair remover.' He met Francesca's glare and tried to look innocent. 'Because, you know, I've been thinking lately, oh gosh, here I am with far too much hair and I just don't want it all. I've got all the hair that I can possibly use at the moment, so I'm just going to remove some, if you'll excuse me . . .'

Jez tried to slide past Francesca, but he wasn't fast enough. She grabbed him by the collar and pushed him back against the doorframe. Her face was so close to his that her nose left a glob of glutchmuck on his cheek. 'Don't expect me to believe that!' she hissed. 'I'm not stupid, you know. I got all the looks *and* all the brains in this family. If I find out you've been up to something, I'll . . . I'll—'

'Francesca,' Jez interrupted, glancing over her shoulder, 'your bath's overflowing.'

Francesca shrieked and spun around. Cursing, she lunged for the taps as Jez made his escape.

Francesca stepped into the brim-full steaming-hot bath and sank down up to her neck. Then she spotted something new sitting on the side of the tub. A tiny bottle. This interested her because she knew a great deal about beauty products. She knew, for example, that it is only worth putting very small amounts of things into very small bottles if they are *very expensive*. She also knew that the more expensive the product, the more miraculous the result.

She scooted up to the other end of the bath and peered at the bottle. 'Beauty Liquid Frighten-ingly Good,' she read.

'Aha! It must be one of those very special products Mum never lets me borrow. She's left it here by accident. I'll just try a little bit.'

So Francesca picked up the bottle of green liquid and squeezed three fat drops into her bath water. She splashed her hands around and a fresh, fruity smell wafted up. Then she settled back with a copy of *Miss Gorgeous* to have a nice long soak.

About twelve minutes later Francesca was flipping the pages of her magazine and peacefully turning into a prune when the bath water started swishing around her. She tried to ignore it but the swirling got stronger and stronger. Then waves started crashing against the side of the bath, knocking her skinny body about.

Francesca glared crossly over the top of her magazine. 'Arghhhh!' she screeched.

Jez leaped up, dashed across the hall and pressed his ear to the bathroom door.

But Francesca didn't say another word. She didn't move an inch. She didn't dare flex a muscle. And WHY was she sitting there, stuck to the bath by her bony bottom and frozen in terror?

Francesca was bathing in shark-infested waters.

Tiny fins circled in front of her. She squeezed her eyes shut, then looked again. 'Keep calm,' Jez heard her tell herself. 'Everyone knows sharks can't get into the bath. It must be an illusion.'

Sharks! he thought gleefully. It was even better than he'd imagined!

Persuading herself that the sharks were an illusion worked fairly well for Francesca . . . until one of the fins dipped down and sharp white teeth bit her on the bum. 'AAAARRRRGGGGHHHH!!'

She flailed about, shrieking. She dropped her magazine, scrambled to her feet, bolted out of the shark-infested bath and pulled the plug. Then she reached for her pink fluffy towel and wrapped it tightly around her.

'Chill, babe. You're safe now,' she told herself.

But Francesca was far from safe. Bath water was soaking into her towel, and mixed into that bath water were three fat drops of Liquid Frighteners.

QUENTIN QUIRKE'S MAGIC WORKS

CHAPTER SIX
THE TERRIBLE TALKING TOWEL

'Hello, Francesca,' said the pink fluffy bath towel, giving her a really good squeeze.

'AAAARRRRGGGGHHHH!!'

'You're all wrapped up in yourself,' boomed the towel. 'And now you're all wrapped up in me. How delightful. I'll give you a wring sometime.'

The pink fluffy bath towel squeezed tighter, and Francesca felt her waist twisting until her front was her back.

'Arghhhh! Help! Get off!' she wailed.

She wrestled the towel to the floor before it could wring her neck as well, then grabbed her dressing gown and fled from the bathroom screaming pink murder.

Jez was just about to look in the bathroom when Mr Lloyd came belting up the stairs. Francesca pointed at the slammed-shut door and shrieked, 'In there, Dad! Sharks in the bath and a talking towel that tried to wring me out!'

'The towel as well? Wow, that's genius!' Jez enthused.

'Stand back, kids. I'll deal with this!' said Mr Lloyd. He barged into the bathroom and stared wildly around, fists raised. But all he saw was a soaking-wet pink towel in a crumpled heap on the floor. And there was nothing worse than a soggy copy of *Miss Gorgeous* in the bottom of the tub. He beckoned Francesca into the bathroom. 'There's nothing strange in here,' he said gravely. 'I think that stuff you put on your hair is seeping through to your brain and sending you a bit barmy.'

Francesca gaped in confusion. Her mouth opened and shut like a fish's. 'But I . . . They must have escaped down the plughole when I let the water out.'

'Francesca, sharks can't get into the bath. Don't be so silly.'

'But, Dad, I—'

Mr Lloyd glared at her crossly. 'And what did I tell you about leaving towels on the floor? Right, that's two pounds off your pocket money.'

'But, Dad, I . . .' cried Francesca again, but Mr Lloyd was already stomping off down the stairs. Jez hung round in the doorway as a sulking Francesca hung up the towel and picked her ruined magazine out of the bath.

'Even if Dad thinks I'm loopy, I know what I saw,' she muttered to herself. Then with the speed of a striking viper she turned on Jez. 'And I know *exactly* who's to blame. You *know* about this, don't you?' she hissed.

Jez tried his best to look innocent, but it was tricky when his mouth wouldn't stop smirking. 'I don't know what you're talking about,' he said mildly.

'Rubbish! You're behind this. I know you are. You and that idiotic Charlie character. I'll find a way to prove it, and then I'll grass you up!'

Jez just gazed at her wearily.

'What are you staring at, bug-eyes?' she demanded.

'Oh, nothing much,' he replied, sweet as cherry pie. 'It's just, I didn't realize you were supposed to let those mud-pack things dry out.'

Francesca's hands flew to her face. 'Arghhh!' she screamed, and slammed the door on him. Jez heard her cursing for twenty minutes as she tried to scrape the dried mud off her face. The Liquid Frighteners had done a great job. Now all he needed to do was get the bottle back. That was easy enough. He'd just wait until everyone was asleep, then creep into the bathroom, grab the bottle and hide it safely away in his pants drawer.

That should have been the last you heard

about the Liquid Frighteners. *Should have been.* Unfortunately things didn't quite go according to plan. The problem was that while Jez was waiting for everyone to fall asleep, he fell asleep.

CHAPTER SEVEN

THE HAUNTED SOCKS

The next morning, as usual, the Lloyds' kitchen table was cluttered with boxes of cereal, toast in the rack, empty eggshells and jars of jam. Mrs Lloyd was reading the newspaper, and Jez was eating a bowl of Wheaties. He had the vague feeling that he had forgotten something, but he couldn't quite think what. Just then, Francesca pranced in, pouting through her greasy pink lipstick. She pulled out a chair and threw herself into it, sighing heavily. Her multicoloured eyelids scanned the table.

'Mum!' she whined. 'These cereals are full

of sugar! You must *want* me to get spots! S'not fair!'

'There's fruit in the bowl, dear,' said Mrs Lloyd calmly.

'Fruit? Just plain fruit?' Francesca whinged. 'But I need those virtually fat-free, wheat-free, gluten-free, dairy-free concentrated fruit-substitute bars — with extra vitamins.'

'Fruit is nature's gift to skin, dear,' said Mrs Lloyd, and wandered off with the post in her hand.

Francesca turned on Jez. 'I don't want you in the house today,' she announced. 'Claudia's coming over to do my nails.'

'Just Claudia?' asked Jez pretend-innocently. 'What happened to Jacintha? Did she finally get sent back to her home planet?'

'Jacintha's working at Mrs Cappuccino's Cafe today, actually.'

'Aw, shame!' Jez smirked. 'You're one witch down. You'll never get your spells to work.'

Francesca rapped her long pink finger-nails on the table threateningly. Much as Jez enjoyed winding her up, he knew when to stop. Those things could do serious damage. One time, he remembered, he'd been a millimetre away from losing an eye. He sighed. 'Well, Charlie's coming over in a minute. I suppose we can go out.'

'Make sure you do,' Francesca hissed.

'Make sure you do what?' asked Mrs Lloyd, returning from her study.

'Nothing,' said Francesca and Jez at once.

Strange thumping noises were coming

from upstairs. Mrs Lloyd frowned at the ceiling. Jez sighed. 'I'll go and check he hasn't got trapped in his polo neck again,' he said.

When Jez reached his parents' room he found that actually Mr Lloyd was looking for socks.

He'd checked his drawers, the linen basket and the airing cupboard. Twice. 'Where *are* the blasted things?' he muttered crossly.

Jez shrugged.

But then they both spotted something red and fluffy sticking out from under the bed. Both father and son lay on the floor, lifted the corner of the valance sheet and peered beneath it.

'Eureka!' cried Mr Lloyd. There were *all* his socks. Every single one. Even the odd ones and the ones that were more hole than sock.

He groaned. 'Well, it had to happen some time, I suppose. You can't just go on taking off socks and kicking them under the bed forever.'

'Can't you?' asked Jez. 'Oh.'

His dad groped around and pulled out two black socks. 'These look OK,' he said, putting them on. He walked towards the bathroom to comb his hair. But with each step the socks gave off a waft of ghastly whiff.

'Phwoar, Dad, that mings!' Jez snorted through his sleeve.

'Hmm, they do rather hum,' said Mr Lloyd. Then he went into the bathroom and shut the door.

Jez hurried back downstairs. He wasn't going to stick around. When his dad shut the bathroom door like that, a pong even smellier than the socks usually followed.

In actual fact, Mr Lloyd was searching the bathroom for something to make the socks smell better. Bubble bath was too sticky. And he wasn't a perfume-wearing kind of guy. Then he spotted something on the side of the bath.

'Beauty Liquid Frighteningly Good. That'll do,' he whispered, grabbing the tiny bottle and unscrewing the lid. He put his nose to the dropper and took a big sniff. The Beauty Liquid had a fresh, fruity smell. 'Yes, that'll do nicely,' he muttered.

He squeezed three fat drops of the green liquid on to each sock. Glancing at his watch he saw that he was four minutes late. He put the bottle back, galloped downstairs and jumped into his shoes.

'Goodbye, all,' he said, kissing his wife.

'Bye, darling,' said Mrs Lloyd.

'See ya, Dad,' said Jez, through a mouthful of cereal.

'You're so embarrassing. It's ridiculous,' tutted Francesca.

Mr Lloyd strolled out the door, whistling.

'Francesca, don't be so rude to your father,' said Mrs Lloyd.

Well, he *is* embarrassing,' Francesca

whined. 'A grown man going to work smelling of your Beauty Liquid. S'ridiculous!'

Mrs Lloyd looked puzzled. 'What Beauty Liquid?' she asked.

Jez's eyes shot wide open. His spoon dropped out of his mouth and clattered on to the table. He suddenly remembered what it was he'd forgotten. He raced upstairs, grabbed the Liquid Frighteners bottle and shoved it in his pocket. Then he galloped back down to the kitchen.

Just at that moment Charlie walked in. 'Hi!' he said. 'Toast! Yum! Mind if I . . .'

Without a word, Jez grabbed his arm and steered him back out of the door.

'Erk! Bye, Mrs Lloyd!' called Charlie. 'Bye, Francesca. Bye, Toast!'

Chapter Eight

FLYING FRIGHTENERS

Mr Lloyd was driving down Hazel Boulevard on his way to Lloyd's Landscape Gardening when he heard a strange sound. It was a sort of scratchy squeaking. He listened hard. The sound got louder and louder.

'This car's due for a service,' he muttered.

Suddenly a clutch of squealing black bats came flying out of his socks.

'Argh!' he yelled, hitting the brakes. The car screeched to a stop and he threw the door open and hurled himself on to the pavement. The bats zoomed past his head and vanished.

'What the . . . ?' he gasped, staring

around. A man was walking his dog, and two joggers passed by on the other side of the road. It was a perfectly normal day. Mr Lloyd stood up and scratched his head. 'Well, I never!' he exclaimed. 'That's the strangest thing I've ever seen!'

If he'd known how much stranger things were going to get, Mr Lloyd would have turned around and gone straight home. But he didn't know, of course, so instead he got back in the car and drove on.

'Morning, Mr Lloyd,' said Miss Berry as her boss stepped into the office.

Miss Berry wore a cream wool jumper with a matching skirt. Over the years she had trained her hair to defy the laws of gravity so that it shot upwards in a big tower.

'Morning, Mr Lloyd,' she repeated. 'Coffee?'

'Err, w-w-what? Oh, right, yes. Morning. Coffee. Hmm.'

Miss Berry peered at him. 'Are you all right?'

'Yes, fine, thank you,' he replied. 'Never batter. I mean, *better*.' He sat down at his desk and tried to think about work.

Miss Berry made his coffee and placed the cup down carefully. 'Here we are,' she said. 'It's quite full. Careful not to slop . . .'

Just then, three things happened at once.

1. Mr Lloyd slopped his coffee.
2. Jez and Charlie burst into the office.
3. Another column of black bats came shooting out of Mr Lloyd's socks.

'Arghhh!' screamed Miss Berry, as they landed in her hair-tower.

'Oh, no,' gasped Charlie. 'Flying Frighteners!'

They watched in astonishment as the bats took off again, dived into Mr Lloyd's coffee cup and drained it completely.

Jez put his hand in his pocket. His fingers closed over the tiny bottle of Liquid Frighteners. 'I am so dead,' he groaned.

Suddenly the bats were on the move again.

'Dad, look out!'

Mr Lloyd threw himself to the ground as the bats made a low pass over his head. Jez and Charlie dived for cover too, as the squeaking black swarm swooped out of the open door.

'Are you OK, Dad?' gasped Jez, staggering to his feet.

'Shut it, son,' shouted Mr Lloyd.

'No need to be like that,' said Jez huffily. 'I was only asking.'

'I mean the door,' hissed Mr Lloyd. 'Shut the door.'

'Erm, OK, on our way out,' said Charlie, taking over.

'What? Why?' cried Jez, as Charlie wrestled him out of the door and kicked it shut behind them.

'Hey, come back!' called Mr Lloyd, but Charlie was already on his Beemo and halfway down Redwood Road, with a bewildered Jez following behind.

'Hang on! Where are we going?' he yelled, pedalling hard to keep up with Charlie (which made a change).

'Quirk's, of course,' called Charlie over his shoulder. 'We need expert help.'

'But Mr Quirk'll be furious!' cried Jez.

Charlie winced. 'I know. But if we don't get his help, the whole town could be terrorised. I'm taking charge, Jez! Putting the frighteners on Francesca is one thing, but this is out of control!'

Jez's face clouded over. 'I won't go begging for help from that nasty old man,' he said firmly. 'We'll just go home and pretend to know nothing about it. Oh, hang on . . .' He screeched to a halt outside the Sheek Street Public Conveniences. 'Here, hold my bike a minute.' He propped his Beemo against Charlie and hurried off into the toilets.

Charlie dropped both Beemos and marched straight in after him. 'Jez, we've got to be sensible!' he yelled.

'No, we *haven't*,' insisted Jez, striding into a cubicle and slamming the door in Charlie's face. 'And I'd like a bit of privacy, if you don't mind.'

'We're going to Quirk's,' Charlie yelled through the door, refusing to give up.

'No, we're *not*,' Jez shouted back.

There was a silence, then . . .

'Arghhhhhhhhhhhhhhhhhh! My bum!' Jez came bolting out of the cubicle, clutching his behind. 'Shark attack!'

'What?!' cried Charlie. He dashed into the stall. 'Holy baloney!' he gasped, staring down at the tiny fins circling in the toilet water.

'I was going to tell you,' said Jez. 'I put Liquid Frighteners in Francesca's bath last night and it made these amazing mini bum-biting sharks. It was brill! But they must've gone down the plughole and got into the town plumbing!'

Charlie went pale. 'This is serious, Jez. What if they've bitten loads of people? We've got to go to Quirk's.'

Jez rubbed his sore bum. 'After *that*, I'm not arguing,' he said.

The boys blasted down Bleak Street and

screeched to a halt outside Quirk's. They dropped their Beemos, shoved the door open and fell inside, panting.

Mr Quirk sprang up from his purple velvet chair. 'Help! Help!' he screeched in alarm. 'Nasty, sticky, smeary, smelly boys in my emporium! Help! Police!'

'It's OK!' hissed Jez. 'It's us. Jez and Charlie. You sold us the Liquid Frighteners!'

Mr Quirk stopped shouting. He peered at the boys. 'Oh yes, I remember,' he snarled. 'What are you doing here? Do you have some more money?'

'No,' said Charlie, 'but we—'

'Well, off you go then,' snapped Mr Quirk. He started shooing them towards the open door.

'We're in terrible trouble!' blurted Jez.

'We need your help!' cried Charlie.

Mr Quirk grinned and began to laugh. 'My, my! That's very amusing. I, Quentin Quirk, help you? Absolutely not. There is no question –'

Charlie took a deep breath. He knew that only the truth would do. 'Mr Quirk, the Liquid Frighteners are loose in the town.'

Chapter Nine

THE BLASTER-TO-BITSER
AND THE B.B.B.C.B.C.C.

'Why, you numbskulled nitwits!' shouted
Mr Quirk, as he chased the boys around the
shop. 'You blundering ninkazoids! You . . .
you . . .'

'You've got to help us stop the Liquid
Frighteners!' cried Charlie, stumbling
backwards as Mr Quirk cornered him.
'There are bats attacking from above and
sharks attacking from, ahem, *below*.
They'll *hurt* people!'

'Why should I care?' Mr Quirk roared. 'I
don't give half a hoot about the idiots in
this town. And as for you two . . .'

Charlie squealed as Mr Quirk's twitching fingers closed around his neck.

Luckily Jez had a sudden brainwave. 'If you don't help us, we'll tell people where the Liquid Frighteners came from,' he yelled. 'They won't blame *us*. After all, we're just kids, right? They'll blame *you*, Mr Quirk. They'll shut your shop down faster than you can say All Vanish Wall Varnish.'

Mr Quirk suddenly went limp. 'You're right!' he muttered. 'My precious emporium! I've been here since 1850, you know! Very well, divulge the details . . . and hurry.'

Jez and Charlie explained all about the bats and the sharks. Though Mr Quirk was still furious, he did chuckle when Jez told him about being bitten on the bum. 'Those sharks are distilled miniature man-eaters, sent over specially from Wallabingbong,' he said proudly. 'And the bats are my own special blend. I call them Biting Black Brazilian Coffee Bats. I am rather a genius when it comes to distillations, even if I do say so myself.'

'Mr Quirk, there's no time to stand here admiring your work,' said Jez (bravely). 'What do we *do* about them?'

Mr Quirk gave Jez an evil look, but then he said, 'Liquid Frighteners have an inbred instinct to group together. So, wherever the bats flock to, the sharks will also be found.'

'And where *will* the bats flock to?' asked Charlie.

'Use your brain, boy,' snapped Mr Quirk. 'The Biting Black Brazilian Coffee Bats live on coffee. They will go to the place in which the largest amount of coffee is being consumed.'

Jez gasped. 'Mrs Cappuccino's Cafe,' he whispered.

Charlie checked his watch. 'It's half ten now. The place will be full of customers. Just imagine . . .'

'I've heard enough,' declared Mr Quirk. 'Come.'

'Where?' asked Jez in confusion. They seemed to be standing in front of a cabinet of glass bottles and jars. Mr Quirk tutted impatiently and counted three shelves down and six bottles to the right. Then, with a knarled yellow fingernail, he gave three sharp taps on a jar labelled Red Herrings. The whole cabinet swung backwards. Charlie and Jez gasped in astonishment, but before either of them could say anything Mr Quirk swung around and grabbed both their necks. 'No one EVER comes into my secret laboratory,' he hissed at them. 'You have to swear not to tell a single soul what you have seen. OR ELSE.'

The boys nodded – well, as best they could while being strangled. They didn't need to ask what 'OR ELSE' meant. They could imagine.

Mr Quirk swept through the secret doorway and Jez and Charlie stumbled behind him, gasping for breath.

'This is where the magic happens,' Mr Quirk announced proudly. 'It is my factory and workshop and the place where I manufacture my most popular potions and experiment with those novel ideas that most intrigue me. This, boys, is my Magic Works.'

Jez and Charlie gazed around in wonder. Old-fashioned-looking machines clanked and clicked. Strange-smelling liquids bubbled in large pots over green flames that seemed to spring from nowhere. A row of test tubes sat on a long wooden bench, their multicoloured contents fizzing and crackling.

'Close your mouths – you'll spread germs,' snapped Mr Quirk as he stalked over to an huge safe that was half hidden behind a tank full of liquid in the corner. He traced a magical symbol on it with one stiff, bony finger, and the door swung open. Mr Quirk reached inside and pulled out a massive contraption that looked like a computer

and a rocket joined together. Jez and Charlie just stared, their mouths still hanging open. As Mr Quirk turned, they shut them quickly.

'May I present the Blaster-to-Bitser,' he announced grandly. 'It is the only one in the world. Invented by a man of great genius: me.'

'Big it up for the Blaster-to-Bitser!' cried Jez. 'The town is saved!'

'Hang on,' said Charlie. 'Bats are a protected species. You can't just wade into a coffee shop and blow them up! No one knows about the Liquid Frighteners. They'll think the bats are real. Then we'll be in even worse trouble. Call-the-police sort of trouble.'

Mr Quirk looked crestfallen. He stroked the Blaster-to-Bitser lovingly.

'For gluey, smelly, smeary little brats, you are quite intelligent, I suppose,' he muttered. Looking regretful, he put the Blaster-to-Bitser down. 'In that case, we shall have to use plan B.'

'Which is?'

'Biting Black Brazilian Coffee Bat Catchers' Corporation uniforms and large nets.'

'*Nets?*' cried Charlie in panic. 'Nets? You mean, that's all we've got to defend our town against hundreds of biting bats? Nets?'

'They are *large* nets,' reasoned Jez.

'Oh, that's all right then!' said Charlie sarcastically. 'Thank goodness for that!'

'Take it or leave it,' said Mr Quirk curtly. He opened a cupboard marked 'Disguises' and reached inside. 'Besides, they are coated with the Liquid Frighteners antidote potion, so all we have to do is catch the bats and they'll disappear. Now, hurry up and get into your disguises. The little monsters may be swooping down on innocent victims as we speak.'

Jez changed into the B.B.B.C.B.C.C. uniform that Mr Quirk handed him. It was far too big and it smelt of mothballs. Even worse, it had no pockets. Knowing that Mr Quirk would kill him dead if there were any more accidents, he slipped the Liquid Frighteners bottle into his shirt cuff and carefully rolled up his sleeve. Perfect. As long as it stayed there, nothing else could go wrong.

'And what do we do about the sharks?'

Charlie was asking as he struggled into his too-small brown nylon uniform with its official-looking B.B.B.C.B.C.C. badge.

Mr Quirk's knees and elbows clicked sickeningly as he pulled on his disguise. 'We'll worry about that later,' he said.

Jez felt queasy. 'You don't know how to stop the sharks, do you, Mr Quirk?'

'I've no idea,' Mr Quirk admitted.

Chapter Ten

Bat Catchers
to the Rescue

'We'll have to run,' cried Jez, pointing up the steep hill towards Sheek Street.

'Run?' Mr Quirk repeated. 'Run? I'm one hundred and eighty-three years old, you know! I haven't run since 1911!'

Jez glanced at the shopkeeper's spindly legs. They looked like they might snap if he tried anything athletic. 'OK then,' he said. 'You'd better have a backie.'

Mr Quirk looked down at Jez's Beemo in horror, but there was nothing else for it. Charlie strapped the bat-catching nets to the back of his own bike, and they were off.

ATTACK OF THE BUM-BITING SHARKS

Jez pedalled hard towards Sheek Street, with Charlie following close behind. Mr Quirk clung to Jez's bike seat, legs waving wildly as he cursed the inventor of the Beemo.

They were a strange sight. As Jez screeched and wobbled to a stop at Mrs Cappuccino's Cafe, he saw that all the customers were staring out at them.

As there was no chaos or shouting or leaping about, he knew that the bats hadn't arrived yet. 'We're not too late!' he gasped, relieved.

Mr Quirk stalked into the cafe and made straight for the counter, where Mrs Cappuccino was busy making vanilla custard tarts. 'Good morning,' he said, trying hard to be charming (which didn't come naturally). 'And may I say how very nice you're looking today.'

Mrs Cappuccino narrowed her eyes suspiciously. 'Can I help you?' she asked, shaking three drops of vanilla essence from a tiny bottle into the huge pan of custard in front of her and stirring vigorously.

'Indeed,' said Mr Quirk, smiling. 'We are from the B.B.B.C.B.C.C., which stands for the Biting Black Brazilian Coffee Bat

Catchers' Corporation. We have reason to believe that approximately one hundred Biting Black Brazilian Coffee Bats are about to descend on your cafe. We are here to catch them.'

Charlie handed a net each to Mr Quirk and Jez. Jez caught sight of Francesca's evil crony, Jacintha Arbuthnot-Smythe, swishing around, clearing tables and taking orders. His stomach sank. He'd forgotten she worked there. He tried to hide his face.

'Pull down your sleeves, boy,' Mr Quirk told him sternly. 'Do you *want* your arms scratched to smithereens?'

'No,' said Jez. He put the Liquid Frighteners bottle on the counter for a second while he unrolled his sleeves. Then he picked the tiny bottle up again and tucked it into his belt instead.

'We need to inspect the premises, madam,' Mr Quirk was saying.

'Is this some sort of joke?' asked Mrs Cappuccino. She plopped three more drops from the tiny bottle on the counter into the custard, gave the mixture a stir and poured it into the two dozen waiting pastry cases, deliberately ignoring the three rather odd-looking B.B.B.C.B.C.C. officers.

All the customers were staring now and muttering. Some of them pushed their muffins and pastries away. They didn't want to eat something from a cafe infested with bats. If there were bats, there might be mice too, or even cockroaches.

When Mrs Cappuccino finally looked up

and noticed this, her face flushed with fury.

'There are no bats here, I assure you,' she said in a loud, shrill voice. 'I run an extremely clean cafe.'

Jez looked at Charlie in panic. Where on earth were the bats? What if they'd already landed, but somewhere else? What if they were waiting in the wrong place?

Mrs Cappuccino stormed into the small kitchen behind the counter and opened the oven. She took out three steaming sticky toffee puddings and put them on the side.

Despite the urgency of the situation, Charlie couldn't help sneaking a look at the puddings. The delicious smell wafted across the shop. Jez shook his shoulder. 'Charlie, stop staring at those puddings!' he snapped. 'The bats could be here any minute!'

Reluctantly Charlie tore his eyes away from the sticky toffee puddings and faced the door, gripping his net firmly.

Mrs Cappuccino pushed the two trays of custard tarts into the now empty oven. She slammed the door shut, to show Mr Quirk just how cross she was. Then she marched back to the counter and looked him straight in the eye. 'I'm afraid I'll have to ask you to leave,' she said firmly.

But Mr Quirk stood his ground. His eyes bore into hers, flashing fire. She stared steadily back. Clearly neither of them was going to give in. The customers held their breath, waiting to see what would happen next.

Suddenly a mobile rang, cutting the silence.

Jez glanced up and saw that the phone belonged to Jacintha. She pulled it from her apron pocket and started giggling into the receiver. Then she noticed Jez watching her. 'Hang on, Francesca, I'll just go somewhere more private,' she said pointedly, glaring at him. And with that she flounced off to the ladies' toilet.

'Wow! No way! Impossible!'

Jacintha leaned against the wall. Something moving in the loo caught her eye. She gasped. Tiny sharks with gleaming fins and flashing teeth were circling in the water! She hadn't really believed it when Francesca told her about the miniature sharks in her bath. But she sure believed it now!

'Jas? S'up?' asked Francesca.

'Come to Mrs Cappuccino's, quick! Those

tiny sharks that bit you in the bath are here. And so is that dorkazoid little brother of yours, in some weird fancy dress. Frannie? Fran?'

But Francesca had already hung up.

Jacintha emerged from the toilet just in time to see the sky darken. Jez, Charlie and Mr Quirk gripped their nets. About three hundred bats hovered for an instant above the cafe.

Then they swooped in through the door.

Chapter Eleven

Attack of the Liquid Frighteners

There were cries of horror as bats descended on people's coffee cups and drained them. The slurping noise was deafening. Then, with the coffee all gone, and the door tight shut, they turned on the customers.

That's when the chaos began. And the shouting. And the leaping about.

'Arghhh!'

The bats scratched around in people's hair.

'Arghhh! Arghhh!'

The bats nipped noses.

'Arghhh! Arghhh!'

The bats nibbled ears.

'Aaaa-yeeek!'

'Go! Go! Go!' screeched Mr Quirk as he,

Jez and Charlie leaped from tabletop to

tabletop, swinging their nets wildly.

Every time they caught a bat, sparks flew and the creature vanished in a spurt of silver steam. Soon the cafe was thick with a silvery fog. Customers dashed around

madly, tables were overturned and cups smashed on the floor.

Jez, Charlie and Mr Quirk swished their nets over the Biting Black Brazilian Coffee Bats until they were all gone . . . or so they thought.

A shout of surprise made Charlie dive across the room and expertly grab the last bat from an old man's beard.

There was stunned silence. Then everyone began to clap.

The three bat catchers took a bow. Jez thought they looked so cool, standing there like heroes in the silvery mist.

'We have caught them all. Mission accomplished,' wheezed Mr Quirk.

'You've saved my cafe!' cried Mrs Cappuccino, hugging them all to her enormous bosom. 'How can I ever thank you?'

'Free sticky toffee pud would be nice,' said Charlie with a grin.

'Oh no,' groaned Jez. 'Look.'

They all turned towards the door. The mist cleared, revealing an amazing (and very scary) sight.

Francesca was standing in the doorway, covered in make-up. But it wasn't her usual pink lipstick and blusher. She had streaks of green camouflage paint down her cheeks. She was wearing army trousers and a tank top with

'Babe' written across it in fake bullet holes. Weirdest of all, she was carrying a big glass jar of gloop.

'Later I will explain exactly who is responsible for all this trouble,' she announced to the crowd, narrowing her eyes at Jez. 'But right now I have a score to settle.'

She stalked into the ladies' toilet. Jez and Charlie couldn't resist following. What was she planning to do? Francesca flung open the cubicle door. The mini sharks were still circling menacingly in the toilet water. She stared coolly down at them.

'So, tiny terrors, we meet again,' she purred. 'You picked the wrong bum to bite! I'll make you wish you'd never messed with me. Prepare to be blasted to smithereens!'

With that, she emptied the gloop into the

toilet. There was a fizzling, then a rumbling. The toilet began to shake. The

rumbling
grew louder
and louder
and louder
until . . .
BOOM!
The
gloop
exploded.
All around
town, water
came shooting
out of toilets,
which was quite
a surprise for the
people sitting on
them. The tiny

sharks shot out too, on the huge jets of water, and vanished in puffs of red smoke.

Francesca giggled with satisfaction. 'I knew my beauty creams and lotions had serious power,' she squealed. 'I just had to mix them up!'

'You made a beauty bomb!' Charlie gasped.

'An admirable invention,' exclaimed Mr Quirk from the doorway.

'Good thinking, Francesca,' said Jez, beaming.

Francesca turned on her brother, and a sly grin twisted her face. 'Thanks. I *am* great, I know. Now do excuse me, boys,' she said pretend-sweetly, 'I've just got to go out there and explain that all this trouble was your fault. You are going to be grounded for the rest of your lives!'

With a cackle of delight, Francesca flounced out of the toilets. Mr Quirk followed her, asking how she came up with the idea.

Charlie sighed. 'That's it then. When Francesca tells, we're done for.'

He was so pale and trembly that Jez racked his brains for something comforting to say. 'Look at it this way, Char,' he offered, 'we're in as much trouble as we can possibly be in. This is the peak. At least things can't get any worse.'

Charlie shrugged. 'S'pose so.'

But Jez was wrong. Things were about to get much, much worse.

Something strange was happening in Mrs Cappuccino's oven.

Chapter Twelve

THE GOBBLINGS

Jez and Charlie shuffled back into the cafe to face the music.

'Ladies and gentlemen,' Francesca was saying, 'I shall now reveal exactly who is behind this whole disaster. The culprits are—'

Suddenly there was a gasp, then a loud thud behind the counter. Charlie and Jez rushed round and discovered Mrs Cappuccino lying flat out on the floor. Strange grunting and groaning noises were coming from inside the oven.

'What was that?' cried one lady.

'Is everything OK?' asked a young man, getting to his feet.

'Stall them,' hissed Jez.

Charlie bobbed up above the counter. 'Mrs Cappuccino's just having a little lie-down,' he called cheerily. 'Nothing to worry about.'

Francesca and Jacintha dashed behind the counter – and screamed. 'Oh, no, she's—' squealed Francesca.

'Fainted, that's all,' whispered Jez. 'Look, take her into the back room, will you?'

'Why should we?' his sister demanded. 'I

bet you've done something else, haven't you? You wait till I tell—'

Suddenly Mr Quirk appeared beside her. 'Just do it,' he commanded calmly.

Francesca took in the frazzled black hair, the long cloak, the gaunt face and the steely eyes. 'Who died and made you king of the world?' she grumbled, but she helped Jacintha drag Mrs Cappuccino into the back room.

The grunting and groaning inside the oven grew louder and louder. The whole thing started to shake and shudder.

Suddenly the door flew open and two dozen mutant

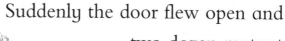

custard tarts leaped out. They sprouted pastry legs in mid-air and landed deftly on their new feet. The fluted edges of the tarts sharpened to points, making jagged mouths full of gleaming teeth. The custard inside looked like yellow pus seeping out of the makeshift mouths.

'Holy knickers!' cried Charlie.

'What *are* they?' gasped Jez.

The mutant custard tarts began to march two by two along the floor and up the wall.

Mr Quirk went even paler than he was already. 'Gobblings!' he murmured. 'The most dangerous Frighteners of all. They don't just bite – they eat!'

The Gobblings reached the counter and began to munch the cakes and pastries on display, chomping loudly. Charlie and Jez stared at them in astonishment.

'You total twit! You absolute twollop!' cried Mr Quirk, eyes popping in panic. 'You should never put Liquid Frighteners into food! The instructions say so quite clearly!'

'But I didn't!' Jez protested. 'I've kept a tight hold on the bottle since this morning. Look, it's tucked safely in here, under my belt.'

Jez pulled out the bottle and held it up.

Mr Quirk peered at it. 'Vanilla essence,' he read, going rigid with fury. *'Vanilla essence?* Explain yourself, boy!'

Jez stared at the bottle in his hand. Mr Quirk was right. The label read 'vanilla essence'. But it couldn't be. Unless . . . His stomach sank. He remembered putting the bottle down on the counter. Only for a second. Just when Mrs Cappuccino was making vanilla custard tarts. Using a tiny bottle of vanilla essence. He groaned.

'I must have . . . It must have . . . Muddled up . . .' he stammered.

Mr Quirk looked like he was going to explode. But just at that moment the Gobblings finished all the pastries and cakes on the counter. They'd grown to at least four times their original size. Custard drool dripped from their mouths. They started eyeing up the people in the cafe.

'Any chance they're vegetarian?' asked Charlie hopefully.

'No, they are not *vegetarian*,' hissed Mr Quirk.

'Well, what do we do?' cried Jez in a panic.

Mr Quirk turned on him, eyes flashing. '*We* don't do anything. *I'm* not going anywhere near them. You're on your own, boys.' Then, for the first time since 1911, Mr Quirk ran.

The Gobblings jumped down from the counter and began to advance across the cafe floor. The customers just stood staring at them.

'Run for your lives!' shouted Jez.

But no one moved. They were all staring at the Gobblings, paralysed with fear.

Jez glanced around. He knew he had to do something, and fast. Otherwise Mrs Cappuccino's customers were going to end up as the Gobblings' main course. And Jez knew Francesca was right about one thing – it *was* all his fault. 'I made this mess,' he told Charlie, 'and I'm going sort it out.'

Before Charlie could stop him, Jez started leaping up and down. 'Hey, greedy Gobblings!' he shouted. 'I'm young and juicy! You wanna piece of me? Come on, over here! I'm brunch, served warm!'

The Gobblings looked at Jez, and their mouths began to drip with even more vanilla custardy drool.

'That's it! Come over here!' Jez yelled, dancing deliciously. 'I'm yummy! Yummy, yummy, yummy!'

The Gobblings changed course and began to march towards him.

Just then Francesca reappeared from the back room. 'Jez, no!' she screamed. She didn't exactly *like* her little brother, but she didn't want him to get eaten by mutant custard tarts.

'Come on, you pastry yobbos!' yelled Jez, swaying tastily.

Charlie began shouting at the bewildered crowd. 'Run! Run! Get away!'

This time the customers snapped out of their trances and ran, stumbling over the broken plates and tipped chairs. In ten seconds flat the cafe was empty.

Charlie noticed Mr Quirk hovering in the doorway. So he hadn't deserted them after all! Charlie stared in disbelief as the Gobblings marched towards his best friend.

What should he do? His eyes scanned the countertop for a weapon. He spotted something gleaming and grabbed it. It was a long steel cake knife.

'Knives are useless against Gobblings!' screeched Mr Quirk from the doorway. 'You'll only create more of the wretched things! You need to stop them from eating! Fix their teeth!'

'Fix their teeth?!' yelled Charlie. 'What do you think I am, a blooming dentist?!'

The Gobblings had reached Jez and were sniffing at his socks, savouring the tasty odour of cheesy young feet. Jez jiggled scrumptiously. The Gobblings' custardy drool dripped on to his trainers. More and more Gobblings surrounded him. Charlie's stomach lurched.

'Do something, you idiot,' Mr Quirk

screeched at him, most unhelpfully.

Francesca emerged from the back room. 'Yes, do something, you idiot,' she screamed. 'They're going to eat my darling little brother!'

CHAPTER THIRTEEN
CHARLIE THE BRAVE

Charlie felt as if his brain was going to explode with the pressure. Then an idea struck him like a thunderbolt. 'Francesca, quick! Chuck me those puddings!' he shouted.

'What?' cried Francesca.

'The sticky toffee puddings. There, on the side, by the oven!'

'Oh, great idea, Charlie,' she spat. 'My darling Jez is about to be eaten alive and you're thinking about food.'

With a start Charlie realized that he wasn't frightened of her. He looked her straight in the eye. 'Shut up and do it,' he ordered.

Francesca blinked at him. Then she grabbed the sticky toffee puddings and threw them across the counter like frisbees.

Charlie caught the puddings one by one. 'Oi, Gobblings, yummy puddings!' he yelled.

'Listen up, gross little Gobblings, eat the puddings!' called Francesca, finally getting the idea.

'Gobblings, I command you to avail yourselves of the boy's puddings!' ordered Mr Quirk.

Smelling the delicious sticky toffee puddings, and hearing the calls, the Gobblings turned away from Jez and began marching towards Charlie. He squealed as they swarmed around his feet, drooling over

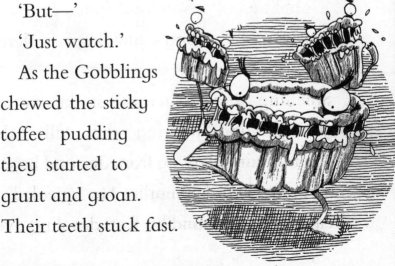

his baseball boots.

'I hope this works,' he said, 'or I'm today's special!' He hurled the sticky toffee puddings into the crowd of Gobblings.

'A noble effort, boy,' said Mr Quirk. 'But those puddings are only a snack to them. They'll be on the loose again in no time.'

Charlie grinned. 'I don't think so.'

'But—'

'Just watch.'

As the Gobblings chewed the sticky toffee pudding they started to grunt and groan. Their teeth stuck fast.

They strained and grimaced, but they couldn't prise their jaws apart. And without their teeth, they were just overgrown bits of pastry with big ideas.

Jez, Charlie, Mr Quirk and Francesca ran into the centre of the room and began jumping up and down on the Gobblings. As they landed on each one, there was a loud crack and it disappeared in a stream of yellow smoke.

'Take that! And that! And that!' they shouted, until the last Gobbling was gone. All that remained was a slippery-custardy-smashed-pastry mush.

They cheered and hugged each other tightly. 'We did it! We did it! We did it!' they chanted, dancing round and round. When they paused for breath, they noticed the crowd of people watching them through the cafe windows, clapping. Grinning, they

all took a bow (causing Mr Quirk's back to make an alarming bone-crunching sound).

Slowly the customers began to venture back inside. Mrs Cappuccino staggered out of the back room with Jacintha.

'Yes, well, I, erm . . .' muttered Mr Quirk, dusting himself off. 'I must get back to my emporium.' It was bad enough that people had seen him hugging and dancing; but hugging and dancing with vile little *children* – that was just too embarrassing for words. He headed towards the door.

'Mr Quirk?' called Jez.

The old shopkeeper turned. 'Yes? What is it?' he snapped.

Jez beamed. 'We couldn't have done it without you.'

Mr Quirk allowed himself a small smile, then stalked out of the cafe and was gone.

Francesca, too, was back to her old self. 'Right,' she told Jez, 'glad you're alive and all that.' She smiled wickedly. 'But now I'm going to tell everyone exactly who's behind all this trouble.' She seemed to have completely forgotten about him being her 'darling little brother'.

Jez panicked. 'Oh, Francesca, please don't,' he begged. 'I nearly got scoffed by the Gobblings. Don't you think that's punishment enough?'

Francesca thought for a moment. 'No,' she replied. She turned to the crowd.

Jez groaned.

'Ladies and gents . . .' she began.

But then a dashing young reporter appeared by her side. 'Miss Lloyd?' he asked, with a winning smile. 'I'm Dean Best from the *Oakwood Gazette.* You are a heroine! Saving your brother's life like that! Keeping a clear head in such a crisis! You must be a truly remarkable young woman. I'm sure our readers would love to know all about you. And we'll put a nice big colour photo of your gorgeous face on the front page – that should sell a few extra copies.'

Francesca beamed and batted her eyelashes at Dean Best. The front cover of the *Oakwood Gazette*! Full-colour photograph! It was her most treasured fantasy come true.

'Erk!' cried Jez, as Francesca grabbed him and gave him a rib-crunching hug.

'Of course I adore my darling little brother,' she said huskily, staring into Dean's eyes as she spoke. 'Which is why I had to think of a plan to save him. When I saw those sticky toffee puddings I just knew—'

'Hang on a tick . . .' cried Charlie.

'Zip it or I'll tell,' Francesca hissed. Then she turned back to Dean and tossed her hair. 'As I was saying, when *I* saw those puddings *I* suddenly knew just what to do. Without *thinking* of my own safety . . .'

Much later, when Francesca had finally stopped talking, Dean interviewed Jez.

'You're a hero too,' he said with a smile. 'You were prepared to give up your life to save others. Would you like to say a few words for our readers?'

Jez cleared his throat. 'Yes, I would,' he began. 'I would like to say that Charlie is a hero too.' Charlie beamed. Jez was just about to explain why when Francesca elbowed him in the stomach. 'Ow! However, I, erm, cannot reveal the details of that for reasons that I, erm, cannot reveal. But I would just like to say that this morning's strange events were not linked together in any way and that they have absolutely nothing to do with Quirk's. Thank you.'

Once the interviews were over, Dean Best left – with Francesca tottering after him. When the boys had helped Mrs Cappuccino to clear up, she made them extra-special celebration blueberry-and-banana smoothies, with straws, umbrellas, sparklers and cherries on sticks. Exhausted, they collapsed into two chairs by the window, where they'd sat only the day before.

So much had happened since then. They'd been down Bleak Street and discovered Quirk's. They'd bought the Liquid Frighteners. They had their revenge on Francesca and accidentally put the Frighteners on Dad. They'd stopped the Biting Black Brazilian Coffee Bats and saved the town from the Gobblings. Jez had been willing to sacrifice his life, and Charlie had saved it. All in all, it had been an amazing two days.

'I've had enough excitement to last me the rest of my life,' sighed Charlie, sucking his smoothie up noisily through the green and gold stripy straw.

'But this is just the beginning, Char,' said Jez, writing his name in the air with a sparkler. 'Just think of all the fun we can have with stuff from Quirk's.'

Charlie spat out a mouthful of smoothie. 'Oh, yeah, great, cos nearly getting eaten alive is such a *laugh*!' he spluttered sarcastically. 'I am *never* going to Quirk's again. Never. Never. Ever. And say you won't either, Jez. Please . . .'

But Jez just grinned at him and drained his glass with a super-sloopy slurp.

MAKE YOUR OWN MAGIC POTIONS!

Quentin Quirk's Amazing Stripy Soup

Stripy and gloopy,
This soup's not for eating.
Turn it this way and that
And it still takes some beating.
The layers won't mix,
No matter how hard you
    shake them.
If potions won prizes
This mixture would take them!

You'll need:

A transparent container or bottle
with a tight-fitting lid
Oil
Water
Liquid honey
Food colouring in three different colours

Mix a different food colour with each of
your three liquids.

Carefully pour the coloured honey into
the container, then the coloured water, then
the coloured oil, and tightly seal the
container. You'll notice that each layer
of liquid is completely separate from the
others. If you shake the container, the layers
still won't mix, and if you turn it upside
down, they'll swap places.

Try adding different liquids like vinegar,
shampoo or lemonade and see how many
layers you can make!

A selected list of titles available from Macmillan Children's Books

The prices shown below are correct at the time of going to press. However, Macmillan Publishers reserves the right to show new retail prices on covers, which may differ from those previously advertised.

Matt Kain

Quentin Quirk's Magic Works: The Purple Sluggy Worry Warts	978-0-330-51022-6	£4.99

Jo Foster

| History Spies: Back to the Blitz | 978-0-330-44899-4 | £4.99 |
| History Spies: Escape from Vesuvius | 978-0-330-44900-7 | £4.99 |

All Pan Macmillan titles can be ordered from our website, www.panmacmillan.com, or from your local bookshop and are also available by post from:

Bookpost, PO Box 29, Douglas, Isle of Man IM99 1BQ
Credit cards accepted. For details:
Telephone: 01624 677237
Fax: 01624 670 923
Email: bookshop@enterprise.net
www.bookpost.co.uk

Free postage and packing in the United Kingdom